KU-697-807

To: Sophie
A magical story
for a magical you

From:

One sunny summer's morning Sophie was playing in her garden.

Suddenly she heard sniffling and crying coming from behind a leafy tree.

4

Sophie
tiptoed closer and closer
to the whimpering.

When she peeked around the tree
Sophie was shocked to see a
little white and purple, sad-looking...

5

"Hello, my name is Sophie, what's your name and why are you crying?" she asked the unicorn.

"I'm Sparkle, and I've lost all the magic colours on my rainbow horn from giving out too many wishes," said the unicorn.

"That's terrrrrible!" exclaimed Sophie. "HOW can I help you get your magic back?"

8

"Well," said Sparkle, "as I become happier colour returns to my horn and when I have all seven COLOURS my magic powers are restored and I can give out wishes again."

Sophie had a think, and a wonder and a ponder...

...what could she do?

"I've got it!" shrieked Sophie.

"We need to do things that will bring back Sparkle's sparkle!"

#1

SO, they tried playing a game of hide-and-seek.

Sparkle wasn't very good at it but because she enjoyed the game so much the first rainbow colour returned to her horn - ruby RED!

ching!

Then they sat on squishy
bean bags drinking hot chocolate
and eating rainbow-coloured marshmallows.
This made Sparkle very happy!

slurrrp

With a slurrrp of her hot chocolate,
brilliant ORANGE flashed up on her horn.

"I know what you need
now," said Sophie...

"...a PAMPER day!"

So they wrapped up in fluffy robes, had their nails painted, and were so thoroughly **pampered** that sunny

YELLOW

pinged back on to Sparkle's horn.

#3

13

#4

Next up on their fun-filled mission was bouncing **UP** and **down**

doing somersaults on **Sophie's** trampoline.

They were having so much fun that Sparkle's emerald GREEN band reappeared on her horn.

#5

Hungry from so much bouncing, the two friends went inside to make **unicorn** shaped cupcakes.

14

There was flour and eggs everywhere when the colour sky BLUE appeared on Sparkle's horn.

There were only two more colours to go and Sparkle was feeling SO much happier, but what could they do to get the last two?

15

"AHA!" exclaimed Sophie, as she remembered the fun fair had just come to town!

#6

whizzed round and round on the last loop-the-loop Sparkle squeaked with suc

They zipped up and down,

16

...light...

...a bright INDIGO band appeared!

There was just
ONE more
colour to go.

17

Exhausted from all the fun the two friends settled down to a magical film and some popcorn. Sparkle was so happy that bold VIOLET, the very last rainbow colour, popped back on to her horn.

"That's it! Thank you **Sophie!**" laughed Sparkle. "You have made me so happy that **all** of my magical rainbow COLOURS have reappeared and I can grant wishes again."

"Now, what wish would YOU like?" asked Sparkle. "I wish, **wish, wish** I could see the Unicorn Kingdom," **Sophie** said hopefully.

19

With a
ZING and a ZAP,
a WHIZZ and a WHIRL,
Sophie and Sparkle soared up,
up, up through the
wondrous rainbow.
Then in a flash
of twinkling pink light...

Sophie couldn't believe her eyes,
she was really there and all because she
had helped a unicorn have oodles of fun!

The End

COLOUR
ME IN